D1577244

About the Author

Les Hopton was born in 1940 in Rayleigh, Essex.
He went through education at Love Lane infants and juniors
then on to Hockley Road secondary modern schools, never
really shining.
Reports said he was a pleasant boy and tried hard. Perhaps
that was it, he never had to try harder, being happy with his
lot.

Dedication

Good Old Boy.	To John Marsh.
Royal Ascot.	To Carole.
The Willow.	To all The old Willow customers.
Watson's Shop.	To Charlie, Coralie, Queenie,
Dorris and Drummer Woods.	
Croquette	To Jean Evans BEM
Old Road Men.	To Ernie Harry and Reggie Cod
'Nipper'	
Fly Fishing	To Bill Phiz
Our Garden	To Betty
The Irish Men.	To all Itinerate workers
Barrow Characters	To Barrow
Lower Farm.	To The Phizacklea Family
Fifty Shades of Green.	To Zoila

Les Hopton

AN EAST ANGLIAN ODYSSEY IN POETRY

AUSTIN MACAULEY
PUBLISHERS LTD.

A CIP catalogue record for this title is available from the British Library.

ISBN 9781785548963 (Paperback)
ISBN 9781785548970 (Hardback)
ISBN 9781785548987 (eBook)

www.austinmacauley.com

First Published (2016)
Austin Macauley Publishers Ltd.
25 Canada Square
Canary Wharf
London
E14 5LQ

Barrow Characters

In the pubs some years ago, were some characters that I
know,
David Rodgers, good old sort, he was rather good at sport,
Played in goal saved a lot, some said the goal was boarded
up.
Darky Fuller known as Zeb, dapper man it must be said,
He went to town on Saturday, in the Nutshell he would
stay,
Don Paske played darts, he made them fly, even with his
funny eye,
He liked to quote Rudyard Kipling, "IF," he'd say and you
were held by him,
He'd stand so close to tell his pun, saying "you'll be a man
my son."
Reggie Cod, Nipper was his nickname, worked for the
council cleaned the drains,
Fell in the pond on Watson's Path, this made some of the
locals laugh,
Charlie Watson heard him shout, rolled him up the bank
and out,
Blue Fuller loved to play solo, banged his knuckles at his
go,
Then you knew he wasn't bluffing, are there rabbits in this
cutting,
If you didn't follow in accord, he said you done me
overward,
Bill Catton wound up Efram Barber, called him monkey
made him lather,
Efram didn't like it one bit, hit him with his walking stick,

Marbles or old Jack Brown, loved to go to Bury Town,
Often he would get quite merry, then returning home from Bury,
In The Willow full of joy, he would sing The Farmer's Boy
Vick Wharfe played cards and got quite cross, especially if he suffered loss,
Once called someone a liar, threw the cards into the fire,
Soapy Nunn was good with an arrow, some would say the best in Barrow,
He worked with Drew and Eddie Crack, making hurdles out the back,
Also he worked in Barrow Wood, at cutting nut stubs he was good,
Gibley Brand and Widdy Wright, a funny double on Saturday night,
Widdy put a spider on the table as a fright, Gibly ate it in one bite,
Phillip Baker and Jack Brown, they fell out one night in town,
Phillip then hit poor Jack, David said "you can't do that",
He hit Phillip in the eye, made old Phillip start to cry,
Later when things calmed down, Phillip gave David a pint of brown,
David flew and got quite dire, threw the beer into the fire,
The fire was really red hot, it went off like gunshot,
Red hot coals flew about, made people jump and shout,
Don Riches the landlord made a stand, "Out you lot you are now banned!"
Richard Baker found religion, didn't care one little smidgen,
Glasses and bottles on the table, "I'll swipe them off because I'm able,
Not one will break you'll see," said he, "because the Lord is here with me."
I don't think that would really matter, down they went with such a clatter.

Again the landlord broom in hand, shouted, "Out you're banned!"

The Bluebells

The bluebells stretch their stems so high, reaching up to greet the sky,
They catch the light before the trees, can spread their shading canopies,
Upon the woodland floor they bloom, before the leaves plunge it into gloom.
Nothing can survive without the sun's rays, that's why they choose these early days,
Their blooms, azure, a sheer delight, seek out between the branches, shafts of light.
There they inspire us with the hue, those special carpets of dazzling blue,
A walk in the woods this time of year, lifts the heart and brings good cheer.

The Cherry Tree

The cherry tree is now in bloom, I see it from my living room,
And as the sun shines on the flowers, I can sit and watch for hours.
The beauty of their petal form and the flowers that adorn,
This tree that I love and adore, for forty years or more.
The only thing is, it won't last long, soon the flowers will be gone,
Like something from Madam Butterfly, the petals will go floating by.
The movement caused by the slightest breeze, shakes the branches of the tree,
Then the lawn and the surround, is carpeted with pink snow all around.
So enjoy the beauty of the cherry tree, in all its perfect majesty,
We must wait another year, for this spectacle to reappear.

Contemplating Wisteria

The wisteria on the garage wall, this year should be the best of all,

The racemes are hanging there in profusion, if it does reach its full conclusion.

A thing of beauty it will be, for all the world to come and see,

The blue, it will reflect the sky, will be very pleasing to the eye

It covers up a bland old wall, and holds your very heart in thrall,

So praying for some frost free nights, to unveil its sheer delight,

But if there should be a frost, then the whole thing could be lost.

Dawn Chorus

When in April the cuckoos sing, they tell the birds it will be spring,

through May and June they persevere, to sing their songs that we may hear.

On every bush and every bough, the birds on mass are singing now.

Here in the garden on the lawn, they herald in the early dawn,

The thrush, the blackbird, and the lark, sing songs that melt the hardest heart.

The swifts, who mostly live on high, sing their song whilst scything by.

The ravens, pigeons and doves too, they caw, they burble, and fracoo.

What symphony they lay before us, the wonder of the birds' dawn chorus.

Fishing

I am not a patient man, so tell me just how I can,
with rod in hand and bait on hook, sit beside a pond or brook.
My one and only wish is let me fish.
I have picked my favourite spot, the carp are rising to the top.
The hook is baited, now I wait, will a fish take the bait.
When they do it is quite hectic, quick now I've got to net it.
Weigh the fish, take a photo to enjoy in albums later
There it's landed on the mat, now I gently put it back.
When it's warm they go cruising by, I've even tried fishing with a fly.
Casting out a good long way into the middle where they play.
When you catch it is alright, they put up quite a fight.
From May to September it is nice, after then expect the ice.
Sometimes I fish on colder days hoping for a few sun's rays.
But all the time to fish I yearn, waiting for the spring's return.

Good Old Boy

We have often heard it said, once some old boy is dead,
"He was a good old boy, never set out to annoy, always had
a kindly word, no one ever heard him say of folk, 'I don't
think I like that bloke.'"
Of John this was so true, now we must give to him his due,
the farm, it was his life's work, never was he one to shirk,
at home with baler and the drill, always had that special
skill.
The combine and the sprayer too, he always knew just what
to do.
With a spanner in his hand, all would say, "He is your
man,"
Tractor, car or a bike, he could mend just what you'd like.
Eighty years he had made, in Gazeley churchyard he is laid,
people came from all around, to see him laid in local
ground.
We were sad, then we were glad, that we had known this
Suffolk lad.
He was 'a good old boy', never set out to annoy.

Hedgehogs in the Garden

We're lucky in our garden, cos we've got hedgehogs. It isn't quite so lucky cos they're eating all the frogs. We know it is the hedgehogs, cos they leave the evidence half eaten they leave their bodies, spread eagled by the fence. We don't mind them eating slugs, and snails, or any other pest, we've even fed them bacon, meat, and pork pie, which is the best, so welcome to our garden. Eat the slugs and snails, we love it when we can tell our friends of our hedgehoggy tales,

So now we're asking, pleading, to all of our hedgehogs; welcome to our garden, but don't eat all the frogs.

Lower Farm

A callow youth not 21, from Essex to Suffolk I did come.

It, I thought, would do no harm, to come and work at Lower Farm.

I lived as family in the house, with Phiz, and Chris, Jane, and Mouse.

Billy too, sometimes a pest, he gave poor Litze so little rest.

The Cridlands, Toolbox, Bill, and Ben, later, it was Pete Whitpen.

Toolbox from east Suffolk quarter, when things went wrong his eyes took on to water.

Ben, a keeper, gentle soul, said Bill was fit to catch a mole.

Peter kept the muck at bay, his wife would say, "I'm lovely," every day.

The pigs were fed twice every day, then the muck was cleared away. We'd plough, cultivate, and sow, then the new crops would grow.

In the fields the work was done, now we waited for the sun. We dug the ditch, and trimmed the hedge, watched the pheasants as they fledged.

The harvest now would be done, I'd get to drive the 21, it was a great big red iron beast, I'm sure I liked it the very least. It would spew out clouds of dust, it was so old, would often bust.

No cab or hydraulics, it was in bad fettle, it was heap of old scrap metal.

The sugar beet, once a wet year, we couldn't get machinery near, so by chance out of nowhere, two men from Ireland did appear,

They knocked and chopped the sugar beet, and threw them into a big heap.

They were travellers and itinerate, and often got inebriate.

Once when they had had a jar, they urinated in the policeman's car, they slept behind the stable door, on paliass made of straw,

And as they came, they went away, like puffs of smoke on a windy day.

The only thing to say they came, were the empty bottles up the lane.

So in my memories of callow youth, there I think I have the proof it really did no harm, to come and work at Lower Farm.

New Life

The buds are sprouting on the hedge, the first young birds soon will fledge,
The twigs and branches with lichen and fungi, through the winter we knew them by,
All the months they had laid looking dead, but now things have come to a head,
The hawthorns were the first to show, a faint green hue does start to glow,
The leaves slowly will be unfurled, to show their beauty to the world,
Magnolia among the first flowering tree, its beauty soon for all to see,
Its delicate flower like flamingos' beaks, from its winter buds it peeks,
Delicate white it shows its face, with pinkish hues at its base,
This is the season, new life appears, promising us all a prosperous year.

On Crattle Hill

On Crattle Hill we parked the car, from there the views can reach afar.
To Thetford across the fields all set with corn, and yellow rape seed does adorn.
Straight ahead is Barrow Plain, where battle was done for how much gain.
The pig styes in the middle lands, stand out like teepees and wigwams.
On the horizon standing tall, thirteen miles distance Elvedon Memorial.
The railway dissects the views, it's Cambridge, Ipswich and Harwich to cruise.
In Barrow Bottom runs a road, where truckers steer their heavy loads, to feed the hungry shipping lines, to Hong Kong, America and the Philippines.
If your imagination is unfurled, from Crattle Hill, you can see the world.

Operation Overlord

In 1944, it was the beginning of the end of the Second World War.

Soldiers massed on the English shore, their aim to defeat the Nazi core.

To Europe they would advance, to land on beaches there in France.

Overlord was its code name, written large in history's fame.

Omaha, Utah, Juno, Gold, and Sword, battle joined with one accord.

On these beaches troops can't yield, in amongst the killing field.

So many men with ships and plane, would not see England's shores again.

So it is with such pride, those who survived could not hide.

We that now do follow on, should praise them all for our freedom.

It's not a thing we want to hide, it's a cause of our great pride. We should all with one accord be grateful for Operation Overlord.

Our Garden

Our garden is a tranquil harbour, where we sit in private splendour.
A seat is there for morning sun, another for when lunchtime's come,
If it's still nice by half past three, our tea we"ll have beneath the tree.
But if it's cool, the garden room, will coy us in and keep us warm,
and in the evening of the day, we watch the birds and animals play.
The sparrows, such a noisy rabble, at the feeder as they squabble, then they swoop into the water, who's in first they give no quarter.
A pheasant and a partridge pair, will clear the seed they've scatter there.
The ducks come several times a day, often getting chased away.
Then in the evening, in the gloom, the hedgehog leaves her secret room.
She hunts the garden, something to eat, a frog, a slug, or piece of meat.
She hides beneath the lowest tree, and there she has her family.
So now you see why it's so nice, to have a garden paradise.

Punting on the Cam

From Scudamore's to Mill Pond Weir, some people do it with great fear,
Balancing on a slippery wet board, praying to the watery lord,
"Don't let me fall in today, don't take my dignity away,"
This is punting on the Cam, whether you are pro or am,
Falling off can mean disaster, also causes so much laughter,
People gathered on banks and bridges, hold their sides and are in stitches,
Amateurs go from side to side, prolonging their ungainly ride,
Don't let your hands on the sides linger, or you could easily lose a finger,
Professionals now a different story, they all go for utter glory,
Sweeping by like driven things, gliding as if on gossamer wings,
White trousers, striped shirt, straw boater, spieling out historic quota,
They tell of princes and academic glory, every one a different story,
Years ago before they came, the locals played a different game,
The undergrads and local boys, would often make so much noise,
Undergrads in cap and gown, from bridge to water they'd jump down,
Up would go a rousing cheer, when a pole from the bridge did disappear,

If someone slipped into the water, it was the cause of great laughter,
If a pole stuck in the mud below, don't hang on, let it go,
Sometimes as a joke, the locals would upend a boat,
People in the water wet, then they'd start to fret,
Sometimes it got quite fraught, and occasionally they fought,
Then the college porters stepped in, they couldn't have this sort of din,
It was getting out of hand, so the ribaldry was banned,
So now it is a time to relax, a leisurely punt along the "Backs".

Grave

Put no plastic on my grave, unless you want to hear me rave,

Or hear me shout and chide, from whatever is the other side,

And flowers when they are dead, don't leave them at my head,

A plant that flowers every year, will let me know you think I'm dear,

A snowdrop bulb or two, will keep me in your heart and view,

Perhaps a rose set in a bowl, that would achieve the goal,

Plastic fades does not look nice, don't put them on take my advice,

So put no plastic on my grave, unless you want to hear me RAVE.

Royal Ascot

Royal Ascot starts today, later on it's Ladies Day.

The car is packed with wicker hampers, don't forget the Bollinger champers.

A woollen blanket to lay on the grass, oh, and each will need a champagne glass.

Ham and salad and bread stick, lets enjoy our picnic.

Smart suits, polished shoes, white shirt and tie, that is what the men will try

The ladies now, a different story, all will go for utter glory.

Each tries to outdo the other, some with creations that hardly cover.

Some quite elegant and unique, others think they are quite chic, when really some are quite grotesque, but they think they are the best.

The hats now come into play, in a hat box stored away.

They can't be worn until the day that would give the game away.

Some of these are an invention, to amaze is their intention.

If you can make the people stare agog, your hat will have done its job.

So off we go to Ascot town, where the Queen may wear her crown.

Bookmakers on the course will put your money on a horse.

Ten to one, six to four, lay your money on the race, and hope your horse is in first place.

So hats and dresses, suits and shoes, it is the end of our carouse.

We've had some fun, enjoyed a lot, our day's adventure at Ascot.

Sydney Nights

It is said of Sydney nights, that the buildings with their lights,
Bring out the wonders of it all, keeps the people all in thrall,
North of the bridge is Kiribilli razzle, offices ablaze with neon dazzle,
The bridge, the arch, a collage of light, the upper most red warns at night,
Bridge walkers with their safety lashing, and their cameras flashing,
Walk the walk both day and night, where they can see this wondrous sight,
On the flat bed trains and cars, their lights like a million shinning stars,
The city now the people gone, the lights in windows still shine on,
Macquarie's, West Pac and AMP, all are alight for the whole world to see,
Cruise the harbour at your leisure, drinking in this special pleasure.

SPRING

Today is the first of spring, oh what pleasures will it bring,
The promise of some better weather, snowdrops have bloomed likewise the heather.
The daffodils wave their heads, in amongst the flower beds,
A blackbird gathers up some straw, and makes itself a nest once more,
New life around us has begun again, encouraged by the warming rain,
The frogs are gathering on the ponds, calling out their croaking songs,
Lawn mowers are now out on show to cut the grass before it grows
The days grow longer without warning, it is so bright in the early morning
The evenings draw out, the gardens call, rejoice it's spring for one and all.

St. Edmundsbury

The abbey gate is open wide, inviting all to come inside.
Take the gardens at your leisure, giving all so much
pleasure.
People say it is the jewel in the crown of this lovely Suffolk
town.
Medevial streets criss cross its heart, the Angel Hill a work
of art. The cathedral with its millennium steeple, supported
by the local people, where Dickens came to take a look,
liked it so, wrote a book, of Pickwick's efforts to become
an MP, and at The Angel stopped for tea.
John Betjeman who said Bomb Slough thought Bury was
so lovely now.
A quintessential English town, so nice no one should put it
down.
The Butter Market and Corn Hill, on market days, with
people fill.
To buy veg, and clothes, sweets and toffee, or just to sit and
have a coffee.
The thoroughfare where we depart, to the new complex
called The Ark.
The buildings are of stark contrast, help bridge the modern
and the past.
So come visit St. Edmundsbury town, you will be welcome,
and not let down.

Sunshine on the Barley

The sun shines on the barley as we walked across the field,
ensuring that the harvest would produce a bumper yield.
It glinted in the avils, in a glitzy shining way, like fairies
with their wings aglow, had just come out to play.
It dappled in the hedges through the swaying trees, it
caught the willow fluff as it wafted on the breeze.
It shone on mayfly wings as they began to hatch, there
really isn't anything like sunshine you could match.
When it shines upon us it lifts our very soul,
Oh sunshine shine upon us. Make us whole.

The Backs Bridges

Magdalene Bridge from Scudamores, duck your head or you'll be sore,

The river they all call the Granta, the Bridge of Sighs is in the mantra,

Thus it's called because some fail, to pass exams and so they wail,

Kitchen Bridge stands alone, crafted from one block of stone,

Trinity and its arches three, one of few bridges that are free,

Garret Hostel, modern concrete, bike to the top it's quite orgasmic,

Freewheeling down the other side, they say is like a sexual ride,

Clare's Bridge is incomplete still, they wouldn't pay the final bill,

A section of a ball it lacks, so they don't pay any tax,

As we approach King's Bridge and College where professors impart their knowledge.

The world is aware of this great place, the Christmas service of love and grace,

Also the wooden chancel screen, reputed the best there's ever been,

Luminaries of great knowledge, all attended this August college,

Is the Mathematical Bridge a myth, no bolts were used to build this?

Not quite true the wise men say, replaced three times as it rots away,

Bolts were always used, as it got the engineers confused,

Isaac Newton accredited with its design but he'd been dead for a long time,
Under Silver Street to the pool and weir, a Lutyens design and quite austere,
These are the bridges along the backs, take a punt ride and relax.

The Irish Men from Lower Farm

The sugar beet, once a wet year, we couldn't get machinery near, so by chance out of nowhere, two men from Ireland did appear,
They knocked and chopped the sugar beet, and threw them into a big heap,
They were travellers and itinerate, and often got inebriate,
They liked The Willow it was quite clear, they drank large amounts of beer,
When they'd had more than their quota, they fell asleep in Snellie's old motor,
Bertie Fitches thought they were dead, found them lying in his shed,
Margie Wharfe sat near the curtain, heard a noise she was certain,
She said to the others, "did you hear that sound?" saw old paddy peeing on the ground,
Once when they had had a jar, they urinated in the policeman's car,
they slept behind the stable door, on paliases made of straw, and as they came, they went away, like puffs of smoke on a windy day.
The only thing to say they came, were the empty bottles up the lane.

The Last Rose of Summer

Is this the last rose of summer? I picked it today.
I can smell in the air autumn is on its way,
A walk in the garden, the leaves on the trees,
The colours are changing, they set me at ease,
The acer, the maple the viburnum as well,
Are working their magic, they make your heart swell,
The colours are vibrant you know it can't last,
The cold hand of winter with its icy blast,
Creeps up behind us and warns us take heed,
New life of spring the winter does need,
So hold onto the summer as far as it goes,
All these things are needed to produce the rose.

The Old Road Men

We didn't have no floods back then, instead we had "the old road men".

There was Harry Brown, 'Nipper' Cod, and Ernie Cooke, each had his own billhook.

Each had a spade tied to his bike, they kept things tidy as you'd like.

They trimmed the grass along the brew, along the kerbs no grasses grew.

They dug the ditches and the groups, drained the water into the brooks.

No trees would hang, giving you a smack, them 'old boys' would cut them back.

If sometimes it rained a lot, they knew which drains would often block.

Even in the pouring rain, they'd be there, to unblock the drain.

Local knowledge did the trick, not someone in a van from Ipswich.

On special days, like wedding or fete, they tidied up, made it look great.

Have we progressed, I think not, I know my taxes cost a lot.

Why can't we have a few 'road men', we didn't have no floods back then.

The Rose

Of all the flowers that are grown, I think the rose should wear the crown.

All the colours that are there, make it far beyond compare.

The many shapes, the subtle smell, lift the heart and makes it swell.

Chosen for a bride's bouquet, on a young girl's special day.

In the house placed in a room, a bunch of roses lifts the gloom.

So in the garden, plant a rose, to enjoy in sweet repose.

The Willow

The Willow sadly closed today, it wasn't always quite that way,
Back in Nineteen Fifty-Nine, all the pubs were doing fine.
Not many people had a car, they didn't go very far,
Perhaps the pictures once a week, for a special treat,
The village fete and flower show, were places to go,
Clubs of all kinds in the hall, a dance most weeks sometimes a ball.
The highlight in summer time, the darts outing, winter it was the pantomime,
There were nothing like night clubs, we all went down the pubs,
Mondays started a little slow, only the regulars would show,
Tuesdays perhaps a game of darts or crib, the old boys would start to rib,
Wednesday a darts match, if it's away a coach to catch,
When at home we had a treat, the landlord provided things to eat.
Thursday perhaps a bit slow once more, not many coming through the door.
Friday things begin to mend, the beginning of the weekend,
In they came very many, to play darts and cards, and shove halfpenny,
Bar billiards and a game of darts, then the solo schools would start,
Saturday some went to town to drink all day, getting in a rum old way.
In the pub on Saturday, all the games came into play,

As the evening drew on, someone would start to sing a song,

The piano now was a mainstay, now get someone to play.

This is what made pubs tick. Then people done their party trick,

When it got to eleven o'clock, then the jollity would stop,

This was the way of pubs back then, weekdays it was half past ten,

Sunday was playing cards day, solo was the game to play,

If you weren't there at quarter to twelve, you could only blame yourselves,

Everyone was keen to play, you'd have to wait for another day,

Six or seven schools played the game, Sunday evening was the same,

Now we all watch TV, get our drink from Sainsbury's,

So you see how things were, what do we prefer, now we have night clubs and bars, everyone is driving cars.

Drink drive laws are severe, if you drive you can't drink beer,

The Willow sadly closed today, part of my youth gone away.

To End All Wars

Poppies were worn on chests today, just so ordinary folks
could say,
Thanks to a generation who gave their lives, so we who
follow should survive,
In peace and love and harmony, but sadly it was not to be,
One hundred years ago in France, the world's armies did
advance,
From Ypres, Flanders and Passchendaele, to end all wars to
no avail,
The killing fields with blood were spread, just like the
poppies it was red,
But still we didn't learn in twenty years, we realised our
worst fears.
At Dunkirk we were in disarray, yet we lived to fight
another day,
The Battle of Britain, Atlantic to, we fought to the death
because we knew,
The aggressor was out to give us strife, and change our
British way of life.
On D-Day seventy years ago, one thousand ships to France
did go,
We stormed the beaches with one accord
Juno, Gold, Utah, Omaha and Sword,
So many died so young were they, that willingly gave their
lives away,
Wear your poppy with great pride, so that we will never
hide,
What our young men all died for, we must never again go
to war.

Victory in Europe

Back in Nineteen Forty-Five, the whole world just came alive,
We had just fought a war, it had lasted five years or more,
Men had died on foreign soil, Churchill promised blood, sweat, and toil,
We came through to win the day, then we heard Mr Churchill say,
"Allow yourselves a small celebration," because you've helped to save the nation.
So the people rallied round, amidst austerity provisions were found,
They arranged street celebrations, all joined in the jubilation,
Trestle tables in the street, all would have a special treat.
Cakes and jellies were all made, on the table they were laid,
Lemonade was drunk in quantity, sandwiches consumed in plenty,
Children all in fancy dresses, young girls their hair in pretty tresses,
Boys dressed up and looking smart, later on the dancing would start.
The grown-ups drank wine and beer, some getting in quite good cheer.
They celebrated all night long, with food, drink, dance, and song, the people had earned the right, to celebrate on V.E. Night.

Watson's Shop

All is quiet on Barrow Green, it wasn't always so serene.

In days gone by, when I came first time, Watson's Shop was in its prime.

A shop, more like emporium, in those days in every village there was one.

Full up with things to sell, green grocers, butchers, bakers as well

You didn't need to go too far, you couldn't, no one had a car.

Charlie was the butcher there, he'd cut and chop and bone and pare.

Dressed in white, looking neat, sawdust scattered at his feet.

Butcher, apron white and blue, slightly blooded by half past two.

In the shop was Coralie, slightly sharp and severe, you couldn't get one over her.

A stalwart of Barrow Church, and Reading Room, very handy with a broom.

No job was too much or greater task, she'd say "you've only got to ask."

Queenie, who was very small, sat at the counter on a stool.

A pleasant lady, slightly strange, she tried to help you with your change.

Drummer Woods, he was the man, delivered orders in a van. Often wore a flat cap, always had it pushed right back.

There wasn't any help yourself, he'd get it for you off the shelf.

Doris was the post mistress, stamps, pensions, licences
she'd process.
Sat behind her metal cage, it all seems now a different age.
Now we all have got a car, do our shopping from afar.
If we had time to think and stop, do we miss old Watson's
shop.

Wisteria

The blooms of the wisteria, are like a scene from a fantasia,
Through winter a bunch of twisted wood, now it's looking
really good,
The elongated racemes like little small buds began, like
curtains now they hang,
Or more like magnificent drapes accentuating their delicate
shapes,
It hangs upon a south faced wall, catching the sun to
mesmerise all,
The pale blue a special hue, does enhance this lovely view,
So once a year for a short time, enjoy the view wisteria
devine.

Woolloomooloo

When I sit at Woolloomooloo, enjoying this fantastic view, my eyes are drawn to Fort Denison, where prisoners stayed for what they'd done. But now every day dead on one, the time is told by a gun.

Across the harbour Mosman Bay, where smugglers had their evil way,

Then Neutral Bay comes into view, a wealthy enclave for the few, then coming left I see the site where president, prime ministers, and royalty do alight.

Still panning left it's Kirribilli, the name inspires or sounds so silly, but office staff toil all day, often for so little pay, this is the way.

I have crossed the harbour to Bennelong, where aboriginals sang their song, the site is now the opera house, where new singers do Carmen, Turandot, and Die Fledermaus.

The bridge now looming into view, it was the vision of the few, started in Nineteen Twenty-Four, finished in eight years or more the bridge is now a shorter course, the first across was on a horse.

The city now deserves a look where bankers like to make a book, like the horse that ran the race, you know they will be in first place.

Now the tower with its views, which one shall I choose? To Botany where cook came in, Olympic Park where we must win.

The Blue Mountains, with their sombre moods, where the blue gum mist exudes.

To Liverpool where ships came from, to bring the massing throng.

St Mary's in amongst the park, tranquil in the city bustle lifts my heart.

Hyde's, Cooks and the Domain bring me down to earth again.

My eyes now take in Finger Wharf, where wool was exported to the north, where dockers toiled with bail hooks, to fill the merchants' order books.

Now it's thank you sir, have you come far? It's 50 dollars to park your car

Below me now, grey ships at Cowper stand, they help protect this lovely land. So I can still enjoy the view, as I sit at Woolloomooloo.

The Elm Tree

Once the noble elm had stood, in hedges, fields and in the wood, but now it's been brought to its knees, by the dreaded elm disease. Along the hedge a different story, a shadow of their former glory, gnarled bark and leaves that wither and die, is what we know them by.

The suckers struggle from the ground, hoping a cure can be found. For fifty years they've held their own, will they survive, it is unknown.

Is it something we've not done right, and helped to spoil this once proud sight.

A stand of elms before I was old, was something wonderful to behold, sadly now the young won't see, the magnificence of a full grown tree.

The Horse Chestnut Tree

The horse chestnut or the conker tree, upon the village green we would see, and in the parks and avenues, they are amongst our favourite views.

In spring there is the sticky bud, then spikes of flowers, white, pink and red. Through the summer the conkers form, when boys would climb with trousers torn, to gather all, and the biggest one, would be used to start the fun. With conker drilled string threaded through, mine is the best, it will beat you. Now will this be in the past, can the horse chestnut last? In the leaf where beetles lurk doing their harmful work, the leaves turn and wither away, it's early autumn some would say. Can the tree survive this pest? We can but hope, that is our best.

The Ash Tree

The ashes, which once were lovely trees, no longer swaying in the breeze. Along the borders they all stand, their branches look like skeleton hands. The leaves they sprout, they really try, only to shrivel and quickly die.

The older trees succumb to die back, the strength to fight they seem to lack. The younger trees we still can hope, through the years will learn to cope.

Ash timber is of top grade, with its wood our tools are made.

It is written in a poem I once read about firewood stored in the shed, ash wood green or ash wood brown is fit for a queen with a golden crown, and ash wood wet or ash wood dry, a king may warm his slippers by.

So we should all be made aware, and hope the ash tree will still be there.

Fifty Shades of Green

How often have you seen the fifty shades of England's green, along the hedgerows, in the park, all the greens of light and dark. I wonder as I walk along, just where did all the hues come from?

The green of new shoots so pale and light, the green of the holly as dark as night.

The green of grass when crushed, the smell, reminds us of fetes and fairs as well,

Who could not love, who has not seen, the fifty shades of England's green?

Leylandii

Leylandii is a man-made tree, for hedges tall, not often loved by all.

It grows so fast, some say it's not right, to block out other people's light.

If it's controlled, and kept in hand, it can keep the boundaries of your land.

Sadly now it's in decline, with dead brown patches it does not look fine.

So we see, some of our flora, is now in deep trauma.

Did we ought to be concerned, are there lessons to be learned?

Should we go back to olden days, see the errors of our ways?

Can we now get on track, by helping nature to fight back?

Croquet

The grass was cut, the edges trim, in our hand a glass of
Pimm's.
The Friday dinner people meet, once a year a special treat.
Here we are with David and Jean, now we organise our
team.
It is again that time of year, when hoops and mallets do
appear.
The game is called croquet, we really need a sunny day.
Through the hoop the ball you tap, there isn't too much
gap.
Take your time, no need to rush, all you need is a gentle
push.
This is a very English way, the gentle playing of croquet.
Then we stop for afternoon tea, on the lawn under the tree.
There's sandwiches all cut nice, homemade cake to have a
slice.
We've played the game and had good cheer, let's all meet
up this time next year.
Thank you David and you Jean, what a lovely time it's
been.